THE LUCKY FISHERMAN

Written and illustrated by
Amye Rosenberg

A GOLDEN BOOK • NEW YORK
Western Publishing Company, Inc., Racine, Wisconsin 53404

In a tiny poor New England fishing village, there once lived a special hedgehog named Spike. Like the other fishermen in the village, Spike was poor. But in another way, Spike wasn't like everyone else: He had the strangest luck. Things just seemed to happen to Spike that never happened to other folks.

Every day, the village fishermen went to sea in their shabby little boats. They never caught many fish, since their lines and nets were poor and worn. Spike said his long, prickly spines were what scared the fish away. That made everyone laugh. Spike was always joking. He had a special happy-go-lucky way that made folks feel good.

One day, while out fishing, Spike felt something heavy on the end of his line. He tugged and tugged, and what he finally found dangling from the line was an old iron kettle.

Spike would have thrown it back, but he thought, "I know someone who could use this."

So on his way home, Spike stopped by Widow Rabbit's house. She came to the door with her children. "I hauled this up today, Widow Rabbit," said Spike. "Perhaps you can clean it up and make use of it."

The widow thanked him and cleaned up the kettle. Then she poured the thin soup that was her family's dinner into the kettle and set it on the stove to heat. When it was ready, a strange and wonderful thing happened: Widow Rabbit found that the kettle was brimming with rich, creamy chowder instead of watery soup—and it was full of that chowder every day thereafter.

The next day, Spike again felt something heavy on the end of his line. When he hauled up the line, all he found was an old hammer. He would have thrown it back, but he thought, "I know someone who could use this."

So on his way home, Spike stopped at the shop of Catwood, the carpenter. Catwood was hard at work. He was cutting a plank with his rickety old saw. "Hello!" Spike called over the *whoosh-whooshing* of Catwood's saw. "Perhaps you can use this old hammer."

Catwood thanked Spike and put the hammer on his tool bench. In the morning, when he returned to work, the carpenter saw something strange and wonderful: There, next to his old tools, hung shining brand-new ones.

Well, two miracles from the end of Spike's fishing line were
enough to encourage the other fishermen to try their luck.

   Soon they were dragging home old boots, rusty anchors,
empty bottles, and other junk, hoping for miracles of
their own.
   But nothing happened.

It seemed that Spike had all the luck. It happened one day that he hauled up an old hat. It dried in good condition, and Spike thought, "Old Woodchuck has no hat. Perhaps he can use this."

So on his way home, Spike gave the hat to Old Woodchuck.
When Old Woodchuck put the hat on his head, gold pieces
poured out of it like rain. Well, that did it! The villagers were
in a frenzy.

So, in spite of a terrible storm the following day, they insisted that Spike go to sea. There was no telling what he would come up with next, and besides, Spike's good luck would protect him. Spike set out to sea.

Soon the storm grew worse and a thick fog rolled in. Everyone feared that Spike was lost at sea, never to return. Widow Rabbit's children began to wail. The widow cried, too. "This old kettle caused all this trouble," she declared. "I'd gladly toss it into the sea if it would bring back Spike." So she tossed the kettle into the churning sea.

"What good are new tools without my old friend?" said Catwood. And he threw his tools into the sea.

Old Woodchuck took off his hat. "I'd rather have Spike home safe," he said, "than all the gold in the world." With that, he tossed the hat into the sea.

Fierce, stormy waves crashed against the rocks, splashing the heavy-hearted villagers and forcing them to go home at last. Spike had risked his life to satisfy their terrible greed, and all the townspeople felt a great sadness.

When morning came, it was bright and sunny. Yet the
villagers were sadder than ever as they trudged to their shabby
little boats for the day's fishing.

They say that a beautiful day after a storm is a little miracle,
and this beautiful day brought a miracle indeed. For there, in
the calm blue water, sat a shining, fancy new fishing boat that
was big enough for everyone. It had new nets, floats, and lines
aplenty. But the best part was that there, grinning from the
deck in his yellow slicker, was Spike himself!

The villagers clattered onto the boat and gave a cheer. They all hugged Spike, even though his spines prickled some of them. From that day on, the village fishermen all went out together every day in the big bright boat, which they named the *Spiny Miracle* in honor of Spike.

Now they were able to catch plenty of fish for everyone, and the tiny village prospered.

Spike never did say just how he got through that stormy day at sea. Some say that a great wave threatened him, but he weighed it down with his anchor. Some say that he caught the *Spiny Miracle* in his net.

Others say that his leaky little boat collided with something in the fog—and when the fog lifted, there was the *Spiny Miracle,* plain as day!

Whatever it was, everyone knew they owed their good
fortune to Spike's amazing luck. And Spike knew that the secret
of his good luck was in always sharing its rewards with others.